Albert Barnes

Life at Three-Score

Anatiposi

Albert Barnes

Life at Three-Score

Reprint of the original, first published in 1859.

1st Edition 2023 | ISBN: 978-3-38231-250-3

Anatiposi Verlag is an imprint of Outlook Verlagsgesellschaft mbH.

Verlag (Publisher): Outlook Verlag GmbH, Zeilweg 44, 60439 Frankfurt, Deutschland
Vertretungsberechtigt (Authorized to represent): E. Roepke, Zeilweg 44, 60439 Frankfurt, Deutschland
Druck (Print): Books on Demand GmbH, In de Tarpen 42, 22848 Norderstedt, Deutschland

Life at Three-Score:

A SERMON

DELIVERED IN THE FIRST PRESBYTERIAN CHURCH, PHILADELPHIA,

NOVEMBER 28, 1858.

BY

ALBERT BARNES.

THIRD EDITION.

PHILADELPHIA:

PARRY & McMILLAN.

1859.

An apology seems to be necessary for publishing a
sermon having so much reference to my own life and
opinions as this has. It is easy to conceive that circumstances may exist which would make it proper for
a pastor thus to allude to himself in preaching, though
they might not justify a more extended publication
than that which is necessarily made in the pulpit.

The following discourse was preached, without
having been written, on a rainy day, when comparatively few persons were present. Some who were
present have expressed a desire to possess it, and
some who were absent have expressed a wish to know
what was said on the occasion. It has accordingly
been written out, as nearly as could be recollected, in
the language in which it was delivered, though some-
what enlarged in the process of committing it to
paper. It contains sentiments which I regard as
important, and which I would wish to commend to
those who are entering on life; and, if it has nothing
else worthy of attention, it has one feature at least
which I would hope may be useful. It will show that
a man who has reached an age at which he can hope

3

for little from the world, may take a cheerful and hopeful view of life—a view which may do something to stimulate those who are about to engage in the struggles, to meet the temptations, and to bear the burdens of life; that a man who has reached the last stage of his journey may see much to live for on earth—much to encourage those who are just entering on their way. At the risk, therefore, of a charge of vanity which could not, I confess, be very easily replied to, but with, as I would hope, so prevalent a desire to do good as to justify what I am doing even with this risk, the sermon is committed to the press.

ALBERT BARNES.

PHILADELPHIA, Dec. 31, 1858.

Advertisement to the Second Edition.

I HAD no expectation that a second edition of this sermon would be demanded. It was not stereotyped, and I anticipated only a very limited sale, and supposed that that would be confined mostly to my own congregation. It is equally surprising and gratifying to me to learn from the publishers that it has received such favour as to justify them in issuing a new edition. The discourse was designed to show that a cheerful view of life may be taken by a man who has come near to its last stage, and who can expect little more from earth; that such a man may feel that there is much that is worth living for, even when he has a prospect and a hope of a better life than this; that it is not necessary that one who is growing old should feel that the world is becoming worse, or that all plans for its improvement have failed; and especially that *temperance, industry,* and *religion* will do much to make life prosperous, and old age, when it comes, genial and bright,—will lead to grateful reflections on the past, and to a happy anticipation of the closing scene.

From the demand for a new edition of the discourse, I infer that men are willing to take these views of life, and to welcome such words from one who has arrived at a period at which he *ought* to be qualified to say something as to what life *is*. I send forth this new edition, therefore, essentially unaltered, grateful for the manner in which the former edition has been received, and as furnishing another illustration of one of the main points in the sermon itself,—that the world will welcome any efforts which are made to promote the cause of truth and virtue.

ALBERT BARNES.

PHILADELPHIA, Feb. 23, 1859.

LIFE AT THREE-SCORE.

O GOD, THOU HAST TAUGHT ME FROM MY YOUTH: AND HITHERTO HAVE I DECLARED THY WONDROUS WORKS. NOW ALSO, ... O GOD, FORSAKE ME NOT; UNTIL I HAVE SHOWED THY STRENGTH UNTO THIS GENERATION, AND THY POWER TO EVERY ONE THAT IS TO COME.—*Psalm* lxxi. 17, 18.

THE occasions are rare on which it is proper for a minister of the gospel to obtrude himself, or his private concerns, on the attention of his people. He has, indeed, like other men, his own private history—the history of his feelings and opinions; his struggles and conflicts; his successes and reverses; his trials and comforts; his hopes and fears. All these are of great interest to him, but in themselves they are of no more importance than the same things as they occur in other men. He may also have arduous labours to perform in his profession, but so have other men in theirs; and I have not learned that the work of the ministry is any more arduous, or more beset with cares and trials, than the path of men engaged in other callings of life. Merchants, farmers, lawyers, physicians, teachers, have their own history, and their own struggles, and I know not why such private matters have any more claim to public attention, or to public sympathy, when they occur in the lives of ministers of the gospel, than when they occur in the lives of men occupied in other professions.

Influenced by considerations such as these, I have never, in the thirty-four years of my ministry,—twenty-eight of which have been spent in your service,—regarded my own work as of sufficient public interest to lead me to preach a sermon on the anniversary of my ordination or installation, nor have I been accustomed to allude to myself, or to my private feelings, any further than occasionally to illustrate some point connected with the work of religion in the soul. This I have supposed was to some extent allowable, for it sometimes occurs that there is no way of illustrating the nature of religion, or of describing the Christian warfare, better than that which is described from personal experience.

If I live three days longer, however, I shall have reached a period of life which seems to me to make it proper to depart for once from the rule which I have prescribed for my conduct; a period not only of great moment to myself, but eminently favourable for taking a view of life as it appears in the past, and in the future. A man who has reached the sixtieth year of his life *ought* to be able to give some views of living which will be worth the attention of those who are starting on the way; he *ought* to be able to offer some counsel which it would be wise and safe for those who are young to follow; he *ought* to be able so to speak of the temptations of the world as to show how they may be avoided or overcome; he *ought* to be able to say something which will encourage the next generation in the duties of life; he *ought* to be able to utter something bright and hopeful in regard to the prospects which are to open upon the world which he is soon to leave—bright and hopeful in regard to the world to which he is so soon to go.

Any young man has a right to ask a man of sixty, How life seems to him now? How has the reality been as compared with the anticipation? How does the world appear now, as contrasted with the vision which rose before the mind of the boy when he sat by his father's fireside and formed in imagination his plans for future years; or when from College Halls he looked out on the world on which he was soon to enter; or when he left the place where he had performed the duties of a clerk or apprentice to go out, cheerful or sad, to make his way in the world? Has the world been what it promised? Or are those visions all illusory and vain? What is there, as seen by a man of sixty, which is worth living for? What should be sought by those entering on the journey? What should be avoided?

At this period of my life, therefore, will you permit me so far to depart from my usual course, and from what seems to me to be usually proper in this place, as to say some things in a plain way of myself, as to what I have found life to be, and how it seems to me now?

Mr. Hume, in his well-written autobiography, says, "It is difficult for a man to speak long of himself without vanity; therefore," says he, "I shall be short." I am sensible of this danger, and I will endeavor not to expose myself to this charge. If I do, it shall be *but once.*

What then have I found life to be? How does it seem to me now?

The FIRST thing which I have to say is, that I have found it to be all, and more than all, that I had hoped; all, and more than all, that it promised. In other words, I have now a higher idea of life *as such*—of the desirableness of *living*—than I had at the outset. It seems to me to be a greater matter by far to live, and to carry out the real purposes of life, than it did when I began my course.

I mean by this, that there is more that enters into the idea of *living—of living in this world.* It is a greater matter. It is a more desirable thing. There are more things to be accomplished; more to interest the mind, to win the heart, to impart happiness; more to make it a serious matter to leave the world at all—to leave it with no prospect of returning to it again.

I know that this is contrary to the impression which is commonly entertained in regard to the feelings of a man as he approaches the period when, in the ordinary course of things, he must expect soon to die. The impression of the young commonly is, that when a man approaches the end of life, the objects which may have been so interesting to him at first must cease to interest him; that, as he has secured all the honour which he can hope to obtain, and gained all the wealth which he can hope to acquire, and tasted all the pleasures which he can hope to enjoy, life can have little to attract him then, or, in other words, that he can see little then which would be worth living for.

That this may occur, I cannot doubt; but it is not so with me, and this is not the view which I now take of living in this world. Life, as such, has now more to interest me than it has had at any former period; more than it had when I looked out upon it in the bright visions of youth, or than it has had at any stage of my progress through the world. There is more to learn; more to do; more *in* the world than I supposed; more to make it a matter of regret that it must be left.

I do not refer here to the things which occupy the attention of so large a portion of mankind, and which constitute, in their apprehension, all that there is in living; the desire of wealth, fame, pleasure. Of the first of these, as a motive for living, I have never been, to my recollection, conscious at any time, nor am I conscious of it now. The second of these I confess I have indulged to a degree which I cannot now justify, and I cannot but feel that I *may* have been influenced by it even when I have supposed that I was acting from higher motives; but I have *aimed* to subdue it, and to keep it subordinate to a higher end, the desire to honour God. The third of these, whatever I may have felt in my earlier days, in common with others as they enter on life, I trust has been subdued by the grace of God, by advancing years, and by the growth of higher principles of action.   When, therefore, I spoke of the world as more desirable to live in than it seemed to me at the beginning, I mean the world as such—as a part of the universe of God—as a place where He is developing his great plans; and when I speak of life as seeming more desirable to me now than ever before, I refer to it in reference to the great objects for which it was given, and to what may be done in securing those objects.

I will specify a few things as illustrating this idea :—

This is a different world from what it was sixty years ago. The universe, if I may so express it, is larger than it was then; the earth is more ancient and more grand. It is true, indeed, that to the eye of an Omniscient Being the universe is the same; but it is more vast and grand as it appears to man. Every sixty years of the earth's history, except perhaps the period of the dark ages, has made the world different; but no period of sixty years has made so great a change as that to which I now refer. The universe to human view is inconceivably more extended. There is not a science whose boundaries have not been greatly enlarged. Many of the most important discoveries in science, and inventions in the arts, which are to be developed in their influence on following ages, have started into being in groups and clusters. Worlds and systems have been brought into view unknown to man before.

The universe *above* is greater. During all that period, the astronomer has been pointing his telescope to the heavens, and penetrating the fields of blue ether, and revealing to man the wonders of the distant heavens; enlarging the universe by all those measureless distances through which the eye has been made to penetrate. New stars have been discovered and mapped on the great chart of the heavens; a new planet as belonging to our system has been found from the fact of its disturbing influence on those before known—a planet on which no human eye ever before rested; a vast number of asteroids, fragments of a larger planet, have

been seen to revolve between the orbit of Mars
and Jupiter; and distant nebulæ, floating
islands in the measureless distance, have been
brought into view, and resolved into distinct
and separate worlds.

The world *beneath* is greater and more wonderful than it was.   The microscope was indeed
known, as was the telescope, sixty years ago;
but it had but just begun to reveal the world
beneath us.   It has not finished its work, but
it has already disclosed a universe beneath us
as unlimited and as wonderful as that above us.
It has peopled every leaf in the forest, and
every drop of water in rivulets, lakes, and
oceans, with teeming multitudes of inhabitants,
amazing us as much by their number, and by
the delicacy, skill, and beauty of their organi-
zation, as the telescope does by the number
and the magnitudes of the worlds above us.
We find ourselves as men standing thus in a
universe extending illimitably above and below
us, as incomprehensible on the one hand as on
the other: boundless space above filled up with
worlds where we thought there was an empty

void, and beneath countless myriads of beings starting into life, and playing their little part, where all seemed to be blank.

Our own earth is vaster and more grand than it was. Half a century ago, the prevailing—the almost universal—belief was, that the earth was created six thousand years ago, in its essential structure as it is now—rocks, and seas, and rivers, and hills having been called into existence as they now are, by the immediate command of God. It began, indeed, to be whispered that it is older, and that important changes had occurred upon the earth before man appeared on it; or that the earth had a history before the history of the human race. I remember in one of the earliest stages of my education, meeting with a remark by Dr. Chalmers, designed to solve some of the growing difficulties from the new science of geology, that between the first and second verses of the Book of Genesis there might be supposed to have intervened an indefinite period of which no account was given, the purpose of inspiration having been first to attest the general truth that "*God created the heavens and the earth,*" or to secure this belief in the minds of men in opposition to the idea that the world is eternal, or is the work of fate or chance, and then, without detailing the intermediate history of the globe, to proceed at once to the main purpose of the volume, the history of the Creation, the Fall and the Redemption of man; that in fact the earth itself may have existed through a vast number of ages, and may have gone through a vast number of revolutions, with which man in his history was not particularly concerned, or which did not bear on the main purpose of the volume—the record of the Fall and Recovery of a lost race. What was then almost conjecture in regard to the past history of the earth, has been verified. The prevailing opinions respecting its recent origin have been set aside. To all that was before regarded as grand in the conception of the earth, there is now added the truth that it has moved on its axis and in its orbit millions of ages; that successive generations of animals have been formed, and have acted out the purpose of their creation, and have disappeared forever; that vast changes have occurred in the waters and on the land, displacing each other, and then peopled again with new myriads of inhabitants appropriate to each, and then again to pass away; that immense deposits of minerals had been made by the slow progress of ages, fitted for the use of an order of beings that had not yet appeared; and that at last man, to whom all these changes had reference, and for whom all the previous arrangements were designed, appeared upon the earth, a being of higher order—the last in the series that was to occupy the globe. With this view of the past, what a different object is the earth now from what it was half a century ago!

A large part of the discoveries in science, the inventions in the arts, and the arrange-ments in the schemes of benevolence that are to affect future times, and whose bearings can now be scarcely appreciated, has been ori-ginated also in this period of the world. The power of steam was not indeed unknown before; but the great changes which it is destined to produce in the commerce of the world are the results of the inventions of this age. The railroad and the magnetic telegraph have been originated in these times. Every science has been pushed forward. Elementary books of instruction have been changed, and those which were adapted to the condition of the world sixty years ago would be useless now. If I were now to begin my education again, a large part of the books which I studied when young, would be valueless. I should, indeed, retain my Homer, my Virgil, and my Euclid; but the books in which I sought instruction in chemistry, and geography, and natural philosophy, would no longer represent the science of the world, or convey correct views to my mind. The books which I then studied belong to another age, and though they will serve to mark the steps by which the advances of science have been made, they will never again be a proper exponent of the true state of knowledge among mankind. I see wonders around me which have sprung up anew. Every river, lake, and ocean is navigated by steam; an iron road is laid down everywhere, connecting all parts of a country together, along which are borne, by a power unapplied when I was young, the productions of agriculture, manufactures, and the arts, with a rapidity and a precision of which no one then could have formed a conception. A mysterious and incomprehensible network, like spiders' webs, is weaving itself over all lands, and making its way beneath deep waters, by which thought is transmitted simultaneously to millions of minds, and is diffused over distant lands regardless of mountains and of oceans. How different such a world from what it was sixty years ago!

In the same time there have sprung also into being arrangements, then unknown, no less adapted to affect the moral and religious condition of mankind. The great enterprises of Christian benevolence, yet to result in the entire conversion of the world to God, have been originated in that time. The Bible was indeed in men's hands, and the gospel was preached, and the power of the press was known, but the serious thought had scarcely found its way into the minds of the friends of the Saviour of bringing the combined influence of these agencies on the widest scale possible to bear on the unconverted portions of the race. Within the period of which I am now speaking, this thought has taken a firm possession of the Christian mind and heart, and the great work of the world's conversion has been entered on in earnest. The Bible has been translated into nearly all the languages of the world; the strongholds of the earth have been occupied as missionary stations; millions of children are taught the great truths of Christianity from week to week in Sabbath-schools; and a Christian literature is spreading its influence far and near over nominally Christian and Pagan lands. Whatever there is of power in these arrangements as bearing on the future, is the fruit of the spirit of this age; and now, in reference to science, to the arts, to the efforts of benevolence—to the world above, the world below, the world in the past, and the world around us, I see a *different*—a *larger*—world than it was when I began to live.

I augur much from this; I hope much in reference to the future. I see that the next age is likely to be more fruitful of great results than even this has been; that it will be an age in which it will be more desirable to live than this has been. I look now on the beginning of things; on the commencement of developments which are to be far more grand and glorious than any which we have seen. John Robinson, the pastor of the Pilgrim Church at Leyden, in his farewell discourse to the departing pilgrims, "charged them before God and his blessed angels to follow him no further than he had followed Christ; and if God should reveal any thing to them by any other instrument of his, to be as ready to receive it as ever they were to receive any truth by his ministry; *for he was very confident the Lord had more truth and light yet to break forth out of his Holy Word.*"* The Bible, in his apprehension, was not exhausted. All its truths were not made

---

* Cheever's Journal of the Pilgrims, p. 165.

known, and there was much in reserve for future times. So I look on the world now. The powers of nature are not exhausted. Her secrets are not yet all explored. The improvements in the art of printing; the applications of steam to commerce and the arts; the disclosures by the telescope, the microscope, and the blow-pipe; the application of light in fixing the forms of things, and of the magnetic fluid in the transmission of thought, have not *exhausted* the secrets of nature. They have opened to us a world of wonders, and taught us to anticipate still greater inventions and discoveries, and not to be surprised at any thing which may seem now to surpass the comprehension of the human mind. We have but just begun to *wonder* at nature—to feel that we know but little about it—that its disclosures are but just commenced. I look forward then to greater wonders in the future, and as I leave the world I shall see opening upon it new inventions, discoveries, and improvements, as marvellous in their nature as those which have marked the age in which I have lived, and as far in advance of what we now see as those amazing discoveries are in advance of what preceding ages had done. You will not be surprised then at what I said, that I have now a higher idea of *life* as such—of the desirableness of *living*—than I had at the outset.

So also in reference to the grand purpose of living—the preparation for a future world—it seems to me to be a greater object, a more desirable thing, to live in this world, than it did when I began life. The importance of this life as a season of probation steadily increases as we come in sight of the end, and see a vast eternity not far before us. The interests at stake grow larger and larger. Those things which ordinarily occupy the attention of mankind dwindle almost to nothing. The earth, as it moves in its orbit from year to year, maintains its distance of ninety-five millions of miles from the sun; and the sun, except when seen through a hazy atmosphere, at its rising or its setting, seems at all times to be of the same magnitude—to human view an object always small as compared with our own world. But suppose the earth should leave its orbit, and make its way in a direct line towards the sun. How soon would the sun seem to enlarge its dimensions! How vast and bright would it become! How soon would it fill the whole field of vision, and all on the earth dwindle to nothing! So human life now appears to me. In earlier years eternity appears distant and small in importance. But at the period of life which I have now reached, it seems to me as if the earth had left the orbit of its annual movements, and was making a rapid and direct flight to the sun. The objects of eternity, towards which I am moving, rapidly enlarge themselves. They have become overpoweringly bright and grand. They fill the whole field of vision, and the earth, with all which is the common object of human ambition and pursuit, is vanishing away!

The SECOND thing which I have to say is, that I have found the world favourably disposed towards those who are entering on life; favourably disposed towards the efforts which may be made to promote its welfare. I found it willing to aid me when I was young; I have found it willing to favour my efforts thus far along the journey. I now regard it as kindly disposed towards young men; as willing to assist them in times of trouble and embarrassment; as willing to commit all its great interests into their hands.

I know that this also is contrary to a very prevalent impression. I am aware that there is a feeling in the minds of many young men that the world is stern and unfriendly; that it is disposed to "turn on them the cold shoulder;" that they who have filled the various professions, and who must soon leave the world, look with an eye of jealousy, if not of envy, on those who are so soon to come into possession of whatever they have gained themselves—who will reap the reward which they would themselves gladly reap, and fill the offices which they would even yet, though in advanced life, secure for themselves: in one word, that they give up the world reluctantly, and regard with distrust and suspicion those who are preparing

to succeed them; that they look on young men
rather as rivals than as vigorous allies, and
commit the great affairs of the church and the
world into their hands because they are compelled to do so, rather than because they have
any confidence that in the hands of a succeed-
ing generation the work will be well done.

That there are such men I do not doubt.
That there are those who are envious, and
jealous, and selfish; that there are those who
are indisposed to sympathize with young men
in their efforts to get along in the world, who
treat them with neglect, and who do nothing
to aid them in their honourable exertions to
start well in life, and who see them struggle
along with difficulties without extending to
them a helping hand, I cannot deny. There
have been such men in every age; and it is
possible that any one entering on life may come
in contact with such men.

But I have not found the world so disposed
towards me; nor is this my experience in
respect to those who have borne the "burden
and heat of the day," and who have toiled for

objects which they have regarded as valuable.
It was not my lot to find that the men who
were in possession of the honours of the world,
or who occupied positions of trust and responsibility, were unwilling to leave them to other
hands; nor has it been my experience that
those who had gone before me were disposed to
throw obstacles in my way as I entered on life.
I early formed the opinion, which I still enter-
tain, that the world is favourably disposed
towards young men, and that all which they
who have filled the professions, and who have
occupied positions of trust and responsibility,
ask in regard to those who are to come after
them, is that they shall evince traits of character which will make them worthy of confidence.
When that is done, they are willing to commit
all that for which they have toiled, and all
which they regard as of so much value, into
their hands.

I began life with no wealth, and with no
patronage from powerful friends. I was blessed
with virtuous and industrious parents, and
entered on my course with the advantage which

was to be derived from their counsels and example. I was dependent on my own efforts. I claim no special credit for this, or sympathy on account of it, for this is the way in which most men begin the world.

I have always found the world kindly disposed towards any exertion which I was disposed to make to put myself forward in life. I do not remember that I ever found a man in my early years who was disposed to throw an obstacle in my way, or who would not have rejoiced in my success. My old pastor, my teachers, my neighbours, I always found willing to help me forward; and what I found in them I have found also in the strangers whom I have met in the journey of life. When I enlarged my acquaintance beyond the limits of boyhood and youth, I did not encounter a cold and unfriendly world, or find that the men who had not before known me were disposed to impede my progress, or to throw embarrassments in my path.

I have never lacked friends; never failed to find a friend when I had need of one. I know, indeed, what it is for a young man to weep when he starts out alone to engage in the great struggles of life; but I know, also, what it is to have tears wiped away, and anxieties dispelled, and clouds dispersed, and the heart cheered, as a man meets with smiles, and good wishes, and new-made friends, and as the voice of public sentiment encourages him to go forward.

As an illustration of this, it may not be improper to refer to my coming among you, and to some of the incidents connected with my ministry here.

I came here a young man, with but little experience, with no personal acquaintance with the manners and habits of a great city, and with no such reputation as to make success certain. I had never preached before the congregation, when I was called to be its pastor. I came at that early period of life, and with that want of experience, to succeed the most learned, able, and eloquent preacher in the Presbyterian Church; a man occupying a position in this community which no other man occupied; a man who had ministered here more than twenty years; a man whose opinions secured a degree of respect which few men have ever been able to secure; a man beloved and venerated by the congregation to which he had so long ministered. I came to take charge of one of the largest and most influential congregations in the land. I came when I was fully apprized that I must encounter from without a most decided and formidable opposition to the views which I had cherished, and to the doctrines which I had expressed.

I found my venerable predecessor already, by anticipation, my friend. He defended my views. He endorsed my opinions. He exerted his great influence in the congregation in my favour, commending me, in every way, by his pen and his counsel, to the confidence and affection of the people to whom he had so long ministered. For six months, the time during which he lived after I became the pastor of the church, he was my friend, my counsellor, my adviser, my example; he did all that could be done by man to make my ministry here useful and happy.

I found a united people. During the six years of conflict which followed—years which are now so far in the past that they can be remembered by only a small portion of the congregation—notwithstanding all the efforts made from without to crush a young man, and to divide the congregation, it never swerved or hesitated. None were drawn away; none among us attempted to make a division. In every new phase of the now almost forgotten struggle before the Presbytery, the Synod, and the church at large, the entire congregation stood by me until the great result was reached which gave us peace.

I found the church at large prepared to sustain me. In the opposition which sprang up around us, I committed the cause—submitting for six painful months, for the sake of order, and because I believed the constitution of the church required it—to what I then regarded, and still regard, as a most unrighteous decision, to the judgment of the church at large. The highest body known in our church—the General Assembly—the ultimate resort in determining the views of our church, reversed what had been done in the inferior tribunals; gave its sanction to the views of doctrine for which we had struggled; and confirmed, by its high authority, the principles which my predecessor had maintained, and which I had endeavoured, as well as I was able, to defend. I have seen evidence in this, I think, certainly in my own case, that the world is kindly disposed towards young men, and that in times of conflict and struggle, when a man needs a friend, he will find one.

And I have found, also, that the world is not unwilling to listen to the truth; and, unless my views greatly change in the little time that remains to me of life, I shall leave it with the firm conviction that truth may be made to commend itself to men so as to secure the assent of the understanding and the heart. I know the natural opposition of the human heart to the gospel, and I am not ignorant that men, under the influence of sinful passions and pursuits, turn away from that truth which would lead them to God. But I have found in man that which, under God, may be relied on in the attempt to convince the world of truth. I have aimed, in my ministry—not now a short one—to declare the whole counsel of God. I have embraced the Trinitarian system of religion, and the Calvinistic system, and have not concealed the features of these systems from the world. I have endeavoured to set forth the doctrines of human depravity, and of the atonement, and of the necessity of regeneration by the Holy Ghost. I have defended the doctrine of decrees, of election, of justification by faith, and of future retribution. I have endeavoured to show to men that they can be saved by no merit of their own, and that their own works will avail them nothing in the matter of justification before God. I have spoken, as I was able, against all forms of vice, against all oppression and wrong, against sinful amusements; I have spoken freely of the theatre, and the gay assembly, and of the influence of the world on the members of the church. That I may have never given offence, is more than a man could have a right to hope; nor do I mean to say that I have always carried the *hearts* of my hearers with me. But I have never doubted that I could carry with me in the cause of truth, if properly presented, the understandings and the consciences of my hearers; nor do I now doubt that the great doctrines of religion *may* be so presented to mankind as to secure ultimately a universal conviction of their truth, and so as to bring all hearts under their control. I am hopeful, therefore, as to the result of my observation and experience, in regard to the power of the truth, and I expect to leave the world with the full conviction that it may be, and that it yet will be, so presented to the mind of man as to secure a universal assent to its claims; so that all men shall receive it, and retain it, with as much firmness as its comparatively few friends do now.

In the THIRD place, I have seen the value of *temperance.* I began life when the use of intoxicating drinks prevailed generally in our country. I was never intemperate; but I was exposed to the temptations to which those who enter on life when such habits prevail, are exposed, and I have seen many of the companions of my early years sink to the grave as the result of habits formed under those customs.

The great work of the temperance reformation, in this country, commenced about the time that I entered on my ministry. I early embraced, in the most rigid form, personally, and with respect to my preaching, the great principle of the temperance reformation—that of entire abstinence from all intoxicating beverages. I have preached, in former years, much on the subject; perhaps, as some may have thought, giving to it a disproportionate importance; and, personally, I have adhered rigidly to the strict principles which I early adopted.

I am now at a time of life favourable, I think, for forming a candid opinion of the principles which I have held, and I have no motive for any bias in regard to the matter. After more than thirty years have passed away in practising on those principles, and after having made so many efforts in my ministry to persuade my fellow-men, and especially the young, to embrace them, I think I am in a favourable situation for expressing an opinion as to their correctness and value.

I naturally now look at the subject *personally*, and *with reference to my public ministry.*

I have mentioned that I adopted the most rigid views on the subject. I embraced the principle of entire abstinence from all that can intoxicate. I have adhered to that principle. For thirty years I have rigidly abstained from even wine, except as prescribed by a physician, and then most rarely. I have never kept it in my family; I have never provided it for my friends; I have declined it when it has been placed before me, and when I have been present where others, even clergymen, have indulged in its use. I have never concealed my sentiments on the subject; and in thus abstaining, in all the circles where I have been, whether of religious men, or worldly men, at home, at sea, abroad, I have seen only a marked respect for my sentiments. However much I may have differed in practice from those with whom I have been, I have never known one thing done or said to give me pain, nor have I found that men, whatever might be their own practice, have been any the less disposed to show me respect on account of my views. I now approve the course, and if I were to live my life over again, I see nothing in this matter which I would wish to change. I am persuaded that the principle has all the importance which I have ever attached to it. I have *lost* nothing by it; I have *gained* much.

I have lost nothing on the score of health; I have gained much. I have had a clearer intellect than I should otherwise have had; I have had more bodily vigour; I have had a calmer mind, and I have had more cheerful spirits. I have had more ability to labour, and I have had a more uniform inclination to labour.

I have lost nothing in public estimation. I have no reason to believe that it has ever occurred that any one has been inclined to regard or treat me with less respect and confidence because of the principles which I have cherished on this subject, and which I have endeavoured to carry out in my daily life. No one has, to my knowledge, ever questioned the propriety of my course, in this respect; no one has ever suggested that it was inconsistent with my profession as a Christian man, or with my duty as a minister of the gospel.

I have lost nothing on the score of usefulness. In looking back now over my course, I cannot believe that I should have been more useful to any class of men by adopting a different course; I am certain that I should have been less useful to many—that many to whom I would be glad to be useful, would have been pained if I had pursued a different course, and would have made it an objection against the gospel which I could not readily have met.

I have lost nothing on the score of happiness. I am certain that I should have added nothing to the real happiness of my life if I had followed the usages which I found in society in early life, or if I had complied with the customs on this subject which formerly prevailed, and which, to some extent, still prevail, among professing Christians and ministers of the gospel. I do not see now—I cannot see—that a different course, in this respect, would have made me a more happy man.

And I cannot forget that by this course of life, whatever may have occurred in other respects, I have escaped dangers to which I should have been exposed, and which might have proved my ruin. I have not lived so long upon the earth without seeing painful evidence that no profession, not even the ministry of the gospel, of itself secures a man from the dangers of intemperance; and I have seen most sad and humiliating illustrations of the effect of indulging in intoxicating drinks even among ministers of the gospel; and, whatever else may have occurred in my life, it is a source of grateful reflection to me now that I have not fallen as they have done; that I have been permitted to feel the confident assurance that as long as I adhered to this fixed purpose I was absolutely certain that one of the direst curses that can come upon men would never come upon me, that of disgracing my profession, and crushing the hearts of my friends, and covering my own name with infamy, by intemperance.

I adhere now, therefore, most firmly to the resolution which I adopted early in my life, and I intend, by the grace of God, to maintain it steadfastly till my death. I see no reason for changing it now; I am certain that I shall see no reason hereafter for doing it. I can conceive of nothing that could be gained by my departing from it; and I do not intend to depart from it. My principles on this point are well understood by all who know me, and I intend that they shall always be thus understood. I commend the same rule to others, especially to those who are in the morning of life, as a safe and a wise rule of life. It can injure no one to abstain wholly from that which is not needful for vigour of mind or body; it would certainly save from that which is at all times most dangerous, and which may be ruinous to the body and to the soul. It would be much for any man to secure at the beginning of life, to be able to make it absolutely certain that, whatever of calamity, trouble, misfortune, or change might occur, one thing was fixed,—that he would never die a drunkard. The rule which I have adopted for myself, and which I have acted on, would make *this* absolutely certain in any case.

I look with equal satisfaction and approbation over my public efforts in the cause of temperance. It was my lot to begin my ministry in a region of country where the usual customs on this subject prevailed, and where alcoholic drinks were extensively manufactured and sold. Within the limits of my pastoral charge, embracing an extent not far from ten miles in diameter, there were nineteen places where the article was manufactured, and twenty where it was sold. I considered it my duty early to call the attention of my people to the subject. I presented my views, in successive discourses, plainly and earnestly. I appealed to their reason, to their conscience, to their religion. I showed what I understood to be the doctrine of the Bible on the subject, and I stated the influence of the practice on the happiness of families, and on the peace, the order, and the morals of the community, and its influence in producing pauperism, wretchedness, crime, and death.   The appeal was not in vain. I found early in my ministry, even where habits had been long established, where property was involved, and where sacrifices would be required on their part in adopting my views, that men would listen to the voice of reason and the voice of God.   I had the happiness to know that, in eighteen out of the twenty places where intoxicating drinks were sold, the traffic was soon abandoned; and I saw, in seventeen out of nineteen of those places where the poison was manufactured, the fires go out to be rekindled no more.   I had a proof thus early in my ministry, which has been of great value to me since, of the fact that *truth* may be presented to the minds of men so as to secure their approbation even when great pecuniary sacrifices must be made, and when it would lead to important changes in the customs and habits of society.

I have maintained publicly the same principles since. I have defended the cause of temperance in every way in my power. I have advocated the principle of total abstinence from all that can intoxicate; I have vindicated the use of "the pledge;" I have argued against those laws which contemplate the *licensing* of that which is admitted to be an evil; I have exhorted the church to set an example of total abstinence; I have endeavoured to show that the manufacture and sale of ardent spirits for drinking-purposes can be reconciled neither with the principles of sound morality nor religion; I have defended the propriety of a law which would wholly prohibit the sale of alcoholic drinks except for purposes of medicine and manufactures. I have endeavoured to show you, that as you would not suffer a powder-manufactory to be set up in Washington Square; as you would not allow a cargo of damaged hides to be landed at your wharves; as you would not permit a vessel from an infected region to come into port, so the true and the safe principle would be to exclude and prohibit forever that which spreads woe, poverty, disease, crime, pollution, and death:—that a community is bound to protect itself, and that no class of men, for private gain, can have a right to scatter death and ruin around the land.

The cause of temperance, as a cause, has met with a Waterloo defeat. The advocates of the use of intoxicating liquors have triumphed. The barriers against intemperance have been broken down. The temperance-societies have been disbanded. The restraints on the manufacture and sale of that which poisons and ruins have been withdrawn. The utmost liberty in the manufacture and sale has been conceded by the laws; and the voice of persuasion, of entreaty, and of warning has almost died away. The community has determined that there shall be no restraint, and that all men may manufacture, and sell, and drink as they please. The floodgates are thrown wide open, and the experiment is to be again made, on the largest scale, to determine what will be the effect of unlimited indulgence in intoxicating drinks. The community has expressed its willingness to tax itself to support paupers, ninety-nine out of every hundred of whom are made paupers by the direct or indirect influence of intoxication; to pay the expenses of building prisons, and conducting the business of courts, and supporting convicts for burglary, arson, brawls, and manslaughter, nine cases out of every ten of which are produced by intemperance,—to bear this enormous burden because there is a small portion of the community which demands the privilege of supporting itself by scattering wretchedness and crime over the land; by breaking the hearts of wives, mothers, and sisters; and by consigning husbands, fathers, and sons to the wretched grave of the drunkard. Meantime the press is silent. The pulpit is dumb. The voice of warning and entreaty has died away. A most fearful experiment is made in the land; an experiment whose result God alone can see.

I adhere now, and shall till I die, to the principles on this subject which I have publicly advocated, and I believe that they will ultimately be found to be true principles, and that the world will adopt them. I believe that the manufacture and sale of ardent spirits for the purpose of a beverage is an immoral employment, and a ruinous waste of capital; that the only safe and correct principle for an individual, if he would promote his health, his prosperity, his reputation, his usefulness here, and his salvation in the world to come, is that of total abstinence; that the practice of licensing an evil in any form and for any purposes— of throwing the protection of the law, for a miserable revenue, over that which spreads woe, and poverty, and crime in the land—is as erroneous in principle as it is pernicious in its consequences; and that the true principle in the matter is that of entire prohibition of that which is "evil, and only evil, and evil continually." I believe that a community would be better and happier, more prosperous in worldly matters, and more religious towards God, where this should be done; and that in doing this, no just principle in legislation would be violated. I expect to die holding that opinion.

In the FOURTH place, I have seen the value of *industry;* and as I owe to this, under God, whatever success I have obtained, it seems to me not improper to speak of it here, and to recommend the habit to those who are just entering on life.

I had nothing else to depend on but this. I had no capital when I began life; I had no powerful patronage to help me; I had no natural endowments, as I believe that no man has, that could supply the place of industry; and it is not improper here to say that all that I have been able to do in this world has been the result of habits of industry which began early in life; which were commended to me by the example of a venerated father; and which have been, and are, an abiding source of enjoyment.

And here—and it was with a view to this in part that I have introduced this subject at all—it seems to me to be proper to allude to what I have never before referred to in the pulpit,—the use which I have made of the press. It may have appeared strange that a man with such a pastoral charge as I have had, and under such responsibilities as have been on me,—a salaried man, employed to do a specific work, and that not the work of book-making,—should have felt himself at liberty to devote so much time as I have done to an employment that seems to be so connected with a private end, and so remote from the duties of a pastor. I admit that the point is one which demands some explanation, and though I have never learned that any complaint has been made in any quarter on the subject, yet it seems proper that once for all—and no better time to do it is likely to occur—I should state why it has been done.

Dr. Doddridge, in reference to his own work, the "Paraphrase on the New Testament,"—a work which, in my judgment, better expresses the true sense of the New Testament, and is a more finished and elegant commentary on that portion of the Bible than any other in the English language,—said that its being written at all was owing to the difference between rising àt five and at seven o'clock in the morning. A remark similar to this will explain all that I have done. Whatever I have accomplished in the way of commentary on the Scriptures is to be traced to the fact of rising at four in the morning, and to the time thus secured which I thought might properly be employed in a work not immediately connected with my pastoral labours. That habit I have pursued now for many years; rather, as far as my conscience advises me on the subject, because I loved the work itself, than from any idea of gain or of reputation, or, indeed, from any definite plan as to the work itself.

And here, as my publications on the Scriptures have had a circulation which I never anticipated, and which I have always found it difficult to account for, it may be proper to state, in few words, the manner in which my attention was first directed to it, and the principles on which the work has been conducted, until a result has been reached which so astonishes me, and which overwhelms me now with the responsibility of what I have done.

My attention was first directed to the subject by what seemed to me to be a want in Sabbath-schools, the want of a plain and simple commentary on the Gospels, which could be put into the hands of teachers, and which would furnish an easy explanation of the meaning of the sacred writers. I began the work, and prepared brief notes on a portion of the Gospel of Matthew, when I incidentally learned that the Rev. James W. Alexander, D.D., then of Trenton, now of New York, was engaged in preparing a similar work. Not deeming it desirable that two books of the same kind should be prepared, I wrote to him on the subject. He replied that he had been employed by the American Sunday-School Union to prepare such a work; that he had made about the same amount of manuscript preparation which I had done; that he regarded it as undesirable that two works of the same character should be issued; that his health was delicate, and that he would gladly relinquish the undertaking. He abandoned it, as I have always felt, with a generous spirit, manifesting at that early time of life, alike in the act itself and in his letter to me on the subject, the same high trait of character as a Christian gentleman which has always so eminently distinguished him. I have prosecuted the work until a result has been reached which I by no means contemplated at the outset.

All my commentaries on the Scriptures have been written before nine o'clock in the morning. At the very beginning, now more than thirty years ago, I adopted a resolution to stop writing on these Notes when the clock struck nine. This resolution I have invariably adhered to, not unfrequently finishing my morning task in the midst of a paragraph, and sometimes even in the midst of a sentence.

In preparing so many books for the public, while under obligation to perform the duties of a pastor in a large congregation, seemingly abstracting time for a private end which might

have been devoted directly to my duties as a
Christian minister, I have justified my course
to my mind by two considerations :—

One was, that I thought that no one could reasonably complain, if I took that time for what
seemed to be a *side-work* before men usually
entered on the duties of the day, and that if
I devoted the time *after* nine in the morning
to the work of preparation for the pulpit, and
to my pastoral labours, I should devote as much
each day to my professional duties as other
men ordinarily do to the callings of life; and,

The other was, that I could in no way better prepare myself for my public ministerial
labours, than by devoting a portion of each
morning to the careful study of the word of
God—the volume which it has been the duty
of my life to explain and defend. The best
method of studying any subject is by writing
on it; and, apart from all idea of publication,
and even supposing that accumulated manuscripts were committed to the flames, I know
now of no way in which a minister of the
gospel could better prepare himself for his

public ministrations, than by spending two hours each morning in a careful and critical study of the Bible. I know of no part of my studies from which I have derived more real aid in my public ministrations, than from the habit thus early formed, and so long persevered in, of beginning each day with the study of the word of God. At the same time, it is not improper to refer here to the *happiness* which I have found in these studies. In the recollection now of the past portions of my life, I refer to these morning hours—to the stillness and quiet of my room in this house of God when I have been permitted to "prevent the dawning of the morning" in the study of the Bible, while the inhabitants of this great city were slumbering round about me, and before the cares of the day and its direct responsibilities came on me—to the hours which I have thus spent in a close contemplation of divine truth, endeavouring to understand its import, to remove the difficulties that might pertain to it, and to ascertain its practical bearing on the Christian life,—I refer, I say, to these scenes as among the happiest portions of my life. If I have had any true communion with God in my life; if I have made any progress in Christian piety; if I am, in any respect, a better man, and a more confirmed Christian, than I was when I entered the ministry; if I have made any progress in my preparation for that world on which I must, at no distant period, enter; and if I have been enabled to do you any good in explaining to you the word of God, it has been closely connected with those calm and quiet scenes when I felt that I was alone with God, and when my mind was thus brought into close contact with those truths which the Holy Ghost has inspired. I look back to those periods of my life with gratitude to God; and I could not do a better thing in reference to my younger brethren in the ministry, than to commend this habit to them as one closely connected with their own personal piety, and their usefulness in the world.

Manuscripts, when a man writes every day, even though he writes but little, accumulate.

Dr. Johnson was once asked how it was that the Christian Fathers, and the men of other times, could find leisure to fill so many folios with the productions of their pens. "Nothing is easier," said he; and he at once began a calculation to show what would be the effect in the ordinary term of a man's life if he wrote only one octavo page in a day; and the question was solved. The result in thirty or forty years would account for all that Jerome, or Chrysostom, or Augustine, that Luther, Calvin, or Baxter, have done. In this manner manuscripts accumulated on my hands until I have been surprised to find that by this slow and steady process I have been enabled to prepare eleven volumes of commentary on the New Testament, and five on portions of the Old Testament, and that the aggregate number of volumes of commentary on the New Testament which I have thus sent abroad, is more than four hundred thousand in our own country, and I suppose a larger number abroad.

I cannot but feel now most deeply the re-

sponsibility of the work which I have done,
and which is so foreign to any purpose or expectation of my early years. I cannot now
recall those books. I cannot control any impression which they may make. It affects
me also deeply to reflect that the sentiments
in those books are most likely to come in
contact with minds through which they will
exert an influence when I am dead,—the
minds of the young. And yet I would not
recall them if I could. With all my con-
sciousness of their imperfection, and with my
firm expectation that some man will yet prepare a commentary on the New Testament
far better fitted to accomplish the end which
I have sought than my own writings are, and
with the feeling that, at my time of life, I
cannot hope to revise them, and to make them
conformable to what I would desire them to
be, I still believe that they contain the system of eternal truth ; that they defend what
is right; that their influence will be to illustrate, in some measure, a great system of doctrines, which is closely connected with the

salvation of men; and that, with all their imperfections, they give utterance to just sentiments on the nature of true piety, and the duties of practical religion. They will disappear from the world as other books have done, and as their author will,—alike forgotten. Yet the *truths* which they are designed to illustrate will live on to the end of time; truths, I hope, to be better illustrated, and more earnestly enforced, by those who are to come after us.

I shall depart from the world, when my allotted time comes, with an impression constantly increasing, of the value of the press, and especially of its value as an auxiliary in spreading abroad the truths of the gospel of Christ. Its importance as an aid in diffusing truth is not yet fully known, and is not appreciated as it should be, even by ministers of religion. Without departing in any manner from the proper work of the ministry; without leading them in any way to neglect the preaching of the gospel, or their proper pastoral duties; and with no purpose on their part to make it a source of fame or emolument, it seems to me now that much may be expected by the church at large from the large body of educated men in the ministry, who, by their training, their talents, and their position, have so much power to influence the minds of men through the press.

In the FIFTH place, I have seen the value of religion, and have become more and more convinced, as I have passed along on the journey of life, that the Bible is a revelation from God.

I began life a skeptic in religion, and I early *fortified* and *poisoned* my mind by reading all the books to which I could find access, that were adapted to foster and sustain my native skepticism. Up to the age of nineteen, though outwardly moral, and though, in the main, respectful in my treatment of religion, I had no belief in the Bible as a revelation from God, nor was I willing to be convinced that it is such a revelation.

Circumstances which need not now be adverted to, but which related rather to the choice of a profession than to any question about the truth of religion, led me to some reflection on the general subject of the future, and to the course which I should pursue in the world. I should have shrunk at that time from its being understood that I read the Bible, and I should equally have avoided any book that would be understood by my associates to suggest the thought that I was a serious inquirer in regard to my salvation. Among them, however, I was not ashamed to be seen reading a book which was in all our hands,—the *Edinburgh Encyclopedia*, then in a course of publication. One of the numbers of that work had an article by Dr. Chalmers, entitled *Christianity*. I read it. The argument to me was new. It fixed my attention. It commanded my assent. It convinced me, intellectually, of the divine origin of the Christian religion. At this day, that article seems to me to be among the most able of the productions of that great man, and to be the best defence of the truth of Christianity which has been published.

But with this intellectual conviction I paused. I formed a purpose on the subject of religion which I then intended should regulate my future course in this world. It was to lead henceforward a strictly moral life; to say nothing against religion; not to be found on any occasion among its opposers; but to yield to its claims no farther. I resolved, to express my purpose at that time in one word, to frame my life, in this respect, on what I understood to be the character and views of Dr. Franklin.

A year afterwards, a revival of religion commenced in the college of which I was then a member, and affected particularly the class with which I was connected. I resolved to carry out at this time, and in reference to the existing religious movement, the resolution which I had previously formed. I determined to say nothing *against* the revival, but to stand aloof from it, and in no respect to yield to its influence. I supposed that I was sufficiently guarded in reference to this, and that no appeal which could be made to me would affect me. A classmate, recently converted, stated to me in simple words, and with no appeal to me personally, his own feelings on the subject of religion, described the change which had occurred in his mind, and left me. His words went to my heart; led me to reflect on my own condition, and were the means, under God, of that great change which has so materially affected all my plans in this life, and which I anticipate and hope will affect my condition forever.

I advert to this here, not only because it was an important event in my own life, but because it has taught me some great truths in regard to religion. My own experience thus referred to has shown me that conversion from infidelity to Christianity, so as to secure an intellectual assent to it as a system, is not necessarily conversion to true religion; that a man may be convinced of the truth of the Bible, and pause there, making no progress ever afterwards; that much more than such a conviction is necessary to save the soul; and

that they who yield the understanding to God
and to his truth, and withhold the heart from
the claims of the gospel, as I had done, are not
safe in regard to another world.   Had I paused
there, as I purposed to do, my whole course in
this world would have been different; my ever-
lasting condition in another world, I cannot
but believe, would have been essentially unlike
what I trust now that it will be.   I have
always, therefore, looked with deep interest and
concern on that class of men, so numerous and
so respectable, who yield an intellectual assent
to the Christian religion, and who go no farther; who admit that the Bible is from God,
but who form a purpose, secret or avowed, that
it shall have no ascendency over the heart.
My own experience has taught me that their
feet stand on slippery rocks; and, urged by that
experience, and by the recollection of my own
danger, it has been one great aim of my ministry to lead that class of men to a better foun-
dation of hope.

This change in my views and feelings occurred nearly forty years ago.   It led to an

entire change in my plans of life, and in my choice of a profession. The time of my conversion to Christ, if I was truly converted, and of my change in my plans of life, was simultaneous. I had intended to enter the legal profession, and had looked forward to it with the ardour of an ambitious mind, nor have I ever ceased to feel a deep personal interest in it. As I view the matter now, it would be to me among the most attractive callings of life, and would be next in my choice to the one in which I have spent my days. But the question, in my case, between the law and the ministry, seemed to me to be one involving no doubt and admitting of no hesitation.

I have never had occasion to regret the change. To that change alike in regard to my feelings, and to my purposes in life, I now look back with more satisfaction than to any other change which has occurred, or to any other purpose which I have formed. If I were to live my life over again, I should desire that the same change should occur again, as most closely identified with my happiness and my usefulness in this world, and with my hopes in the future life.

I am now more firmly, and I trust more intelligently, impressed with the truth of Christianity, and with the belief that the Bible is a revelation from God, than I was when that change occurred. That I saw difficulties in the scheme of Christianity, and in the Bible, then; that I have seen them since; that I see them now, I do not deny; nor do I expect to reach a position in this world where objections could not be suggested on the whole subject of religion which I should not be able to solve. But I have spent more than thirty years in a close study of the Sacred Scriptures, and no small part of my inquiries has had reference to the difficulties which were suggested to my mind by my early skepticism, and to those which to a mind naturally inclined to unbelief have been suggested since. I do not mean to say that all those difficulties have been removed. But I have found that, on a close examination, not a few of those which at first perplexed me have silently disappeared; that a large part of those which have been since suggested have vanished also; and that, in the mean time, the evidences of the truth of the Bible have, in my apprehension, become stronger and stronger. Thus a large part of the difficulties which once perplexed me have vanished entirely; a portion of them have taken their place by the side of undisputed *facts* actually existing in the world, in reference to which there are the same difficult questions to be answered as in regard to the difficulties in the Bible, and which do not pertain, therefore, peculiarly to revelation, and about which, as a believer in revelation, I give myself no special perplexity or trouble. My experience in the matter has led me to hope and believe that a longer and more patient study would in a similar manner remove all the difficulties which I now see in the Christian system, and make what now appears to be inconsistent harmonious, and what is now dark clear. I come, therefore, in this respect, with the language of encouragement to those who are now just entering on their Christian way, and who find their minds poisoned by skepticism, and their course impeded by difficulties. Time, patience, study, reflection, prayer, suggestions from within and from without, accompanied by the influences of the Divine Spirit, will remove most of those difficulties, and will leave at last only those which belong, not peculiarly to the Bible, but to the mysterious order of things around us; to those which lie wholly beyond the reach of our present powers, and which must be left for solution to an eternal world. It should never be forgotten that these great subjects are to engross our thoughts forever, and that it was needful that the universe should be so made as to give *eternal* occupation to the intellect and the heart. We are in the very infancy of our being now, and it would make the heaven before us a blank if there were no subjects demanding our thoughts, and fitted to give occupation to mind, which we could not grasp and explain now. I have never intended to turn away from *any* difficulty which has come in my path on the subject of religion; I have never designed to evade an objection, come from what quarter it might; I have never refused as a personal matter to listen to any suggestion which would seem to militate against the truth of religion, and to examine it. I can have no object in being deceived, or in deceiving others; I have as much personal interest as any other man can have in the question whether Christianity is true or false. I say now, therefore, that I am more firmly and more intelligently convinced of the truth of the Bible than I was at twenty-one years of age; that the difficulties which I then saw have been silently and gradually melting away; and that I now perceive scarcely any which I do not see existing with equal force in the analogy of nature, or which are not such as lie beyond the powers of man as yet developed, and which properly pertain to another world.

The language of the late Professor Stuart, of Andover, well describes my own experience on this subject:—" In the early part of my Biblical studies, some thirty to thirty-five years ago," says he, " when I first began the critical investigation of the Scriptures, doubts

and difficulties started up on every side, like
the armed men whom Cadmus is fabled to
have raised up. Time, patience, continued
study, a better acquaintance with the original
scriptural languages, and the countries where
the sacred books were written, have scattered
to the winds nearly all those doubts. I meet,
indeed," says he, " with difficulties still, which
I cannot solve at once ; with some where even
repeated efforts have not solved them. But I
quiet myself by calling to mind that hosts of
other difficulties, once apparently to me as
formidable as these, have been removed, and
have disappeared from the circle of my trou-
bled vision. Why may I not hope, then, as
to the difficulties that remain ?"*

I now declare to you solemnly, in this public
manner, that I have no hope of the immortality of the soul, or of future happiness, except that which is found in the gospel of
Christ. I have seen no evidence—I now see
none—of the immortality of the soul as derived from human reasoning which would be

---

* Canon of the Old Testament, p. 18.

satisfactory to my mind; and my belief that the soul will exist forever is founded on the fact that "life and immortality are brought to light through the gospel." The reasoning of Plato on the subject, in the Phædo, has done nothing to convince me on that point; nor have I met with any reasoning, apart from the statements of the Bible, which would convince me, or which would give support and consolation to my anxious mind when I think on this great subject. And, in the same manner, I declare to you that I have no hope of heaven except that which is derived from what the Saviour has done for lost sinners,—a hope founded solely on his atonement; his merit; his intercession. I can adopt now, as expressing the whole of my belief and my hope, the sentiment which my venerable preceptor, Dr. Alexander, is understood to have expressed in his last moments, as constituting the "whole of his theology:"—"This is a faithful saying, and worthy of all acceptation, that Christ Jesus came into the world to save sinners;" and though I fear that in death I

should be compelled, much more than he
needed to do, to mingle with this expression
of my faith the language which our great
statesman* is said to have uttered in his
dying moments, "Lord, I believe, help thou
mine unbelief," yet still this *is* my faith, and
this *is* my hope. I have no other. I desire
no other.

I have thus submitted to you what I wished
to express on an occasion that is to me of so
much interest. I could turn the table—I
could give you the *obverse* of this—I could
recount errors and short-comings and imperfections in my life, of which I am now deeply
conscious, and which will be to me a source of
regret to the end of my days; but these do
not pertain to an occasion like this. They
belong to the "closet,"—the place where a
man is alone with God, and where he seeks
for pardon through the blood of the atonement.

I enter now on what I must regard as the
last stage of my existence on earth. I have

* Daniel Webster.

reached the summit of life. I cannot expect or hope to rise higher. I have come to the top of the hill, and I have found there, as one sometimes does when he ascends a mountain, a little spot which seems to me to be level ground—a small area of table-land—a plateau—that spreads out a little distance around me. If I am permitted to walk for a few years on that plateau—that table-land—that level spot—it is all that I can now hope for. I can look for no greater degree of vigour of body or of mind; for no greater ability to labour. That little spot of level ground which I seem to have found on the summit, spreads out before me with much that is inviting. I cannot deny that I would, on many accounts, love to linger there, and extend my walk further than I can reasonably hope that I shall be permitted to do. But I desire not to forget that though this little spot *seems* to me to be level, yet if I continue to walk over it for a little time I must find it soon begin to slope in the other direction, or that I may soon come to a precipice down which I shall suddenly fall to rise no more. At all events, I know that I *shall*—that I *must*—soon come to a place where it will begin to descend; nor would I forget that the descent must be much more steep than the rise has been, and that the hill which has been of so easy a grade on the one side may be on the other a most steep declivity, or that from the top of the hill which it has required so many years to climb, the descent to the bottom may occur in a moment.

Permit me to say that I am, at this period of my life, *hopeful* in regard to the world, to truth, to religion, to liberty, to the advancement of the race. The world is growing better; not worse. It is better now than it was sixty years ago; it is becoming better every year, every month, every day. In its progress society takes hold of all that is valuable, or that constitutes real improvement, and will not let it die. That which is worthless is superseded by that which is useful; that which is injurious and wrong is dropped by the way; that which goes permanently into the good order of the world alone is retained. There is more love of truth than there was sixty years ago; there is more science; there are more of the comforts of life; there is more freedom; there is more religion. There will be more in the next age than there is now; and so on to the end of time. Christianity never had so firm a hold on the intelligent faith of mankind as it has now. It will have a firmer hold on the next age, and will extend its triumphs until the world—the whole world—shall be converted to the Saviour. Old men often feel that the world is growing worse. I have not that feeling now; by the grace of God, I shall never have it. I *intend* to hold on to the conviction which I now have at this mature period of my life, that the world is becoming better; I design to cherish this conviction when I die. I do not despond or despair in regard to men; to the church; to my country; to the cause of humanity; to the cause of freedom. I believe that the whole world will be converted to truth and righteousness; and if I should be spared to that period when I should be willing to fill up that part of the text which I have omitted now, and to speak of myself as "*old and gray-headed*," I intend that there shall be at least *one* aged man who will take a cheerful and hopeful view of the world as he leaves it. Happy will he be who shall live in those times that are coming upon the world, and who shall see the full development of the things now springing up on the earth which tend to the recovery and redemption of the race! It is much to have lived sixty years in a period of the world like that which is now past; it will be a much greater thing to live in those brighter and happier years which are soon to follow. With my views of heaven, I can indeed *envy*—even if envy were ever proper—no one who is to remain on the earth; and yet there are scenes to occur here below which one who cherishes such views as I do, and who is about to leave the world even with the hope of heaven, could not but desire to witness. I would be glad if these remarks might show you that as men advance in life it is not *necessary*, though it is so *common*, to feel that the world is becoming worse; and that a man who is soon to leave the earth himself *may* take such a view of human affairs as to enable him to utter a cheering word to those who are entering on the struggles of life, and show them that there is much for the church to hope for, much to live and labour for.

Finally. I am personally *hopeful* in regard to the future world. I cherish the hope that I may reach heaven; and that, having been so long a professor of religion, I may be "kept from falling," and be preserved unto the eternal kingdom of the Redeemer. On this point, pertaining so much to a man's private feelings, and to his personal relations to God, it is not proper that I should in a public manner say more than this. But I know how a man *ought* to feel who has reached the sixtieth year of his life; I know how a Christian minister ought to preach,—what such a man should live for; what he should aim to do; what spirit he should be of. I know how a man *ought* to live who feels that he is rapidly approaching heaven—how he ought to labour; to pray; to wait; to hope;

to be patient; how he ought to be found at the post of duty, and to gird himself for the last conflict. I shall accomplish what I ought to accomplish; shall live as I ought to live; shall be faithful as a pastor as I ought to be faithful; shall preach as I ought to preach; and shall die with the bright anticipations which a Christian man ought to possess, and which I most earnestly desire may be mine when I die, very much as I am sustained by your prayers. Is it improper, then, to ask your prayers, that "I may finish my course with joy, and the ministry which I have received of the Lord Jesus, to testify the gospel of the grace of God!"